The Croatan Woods Vol I in

The Adventures of Benny and Flash

For Marie

This book is a work of fiction. Names, characters,
places and incidents are either the product of the
author's imagination, or are used fictitiously.

ISBN 978-0-9974580-0-8
Library of Congress Control Number: 2016913521

The Adventures of Benny and Flash

Vol I – The Croatan Woods

Kat Hoke

One White Foot Publishing
New Bern NC

Contents

Chapter 1
The Tree

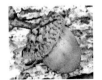 Long, long ago, deep in the Croatan Woods of North Carolina, a tiny acorn tumbled to the ground. It slept quietly, unnoticed, as the weeks passed by.

Underground, the acorn sunk its feet deep into the soft, rich soil of the forest floor.

Suddenly, a tiny shoot popped up through the ground. The miracle of life had begun! Leaves opened to embrace the warm sunshine.

The rains fell, the sun shone, and inch by inch, the little acorn, now a young tree, grew up and up toward the big blue sky.

In those days so long ago, the Croatan was a mighty forest, filled with many kinds of trees: poplars and magnolias, redbuds and dogwoods and pines.

There were many kinds of creatures too; bugs and frogs, rabbits and deer, black bears and even people made their homes in the Croatan.

Each year, the little tree watched the world around it change, slowly at first, and then faster as the seasons came and went.

The tree watched as the Neusiok Indians traveled down the dirt paths that snaked through the forest, on their way to a hunt, or carrying baskets of corn on their heads. . .

. . . and it saw those same Indians kidnap two important men from the small village of New Bern, and take them far off, into the woods.

The tree didn't know what became of those men, but there were many years of war in the Croatan, until finally there were no Neusiok Indians left.

The seasons passed; winter followed autumn, and summer

followed spring, and the tree grew and grew.

Several years had come and gone, when one day the tree saw a group of men sneaking silently down those same dirt paths, carrying a  large canvas bag over their shoulders. These men looked very different from the ones the tree had seen before. They dug a deep hole, dropped the bag down into it, covered it with dirt, and rolled a large stone over the top.

The tree never learned what was in that bag, but it heard the men sing a song as they finished their strange task, *"Ho ho ho and a bottle of rum. . ."*

Decades passed, and many more people could be seen traveling through the woods. One night, a small group of men camped beneath the tree's branches. These men talked of war, freedom, and a man named George Washington.

Many more years flowed down the river of time, and the tree grew and grew.

Another war brought still more men, some of them sailors moving quickly down the Neuse in their tall ships; some of them soldiers camping beneath the tree's green leaf canopy.

They called this one a "Civil War", but from what the tree could see, there was nothing civil about it.

Years had now turned to decades, and decades to centuries. The little acorn had grown into a mighty oak tree, more than one hundred feet tall. From such a high vantage point, the tree could see that, sadly, little was left of the once great Croatan. Much of the forest had been cut down to build businesses, houses, and ships.

Year after year, the sound of lumber mill saws had echoed in the woods day and night. The sound of train whistles echoed, too, as they passed through the forest carrying that lumber to Raleigh and cities beyond.

One night, a ferocious hurricane blew in from the sea. The storm was so big, it covered more than three hundred square miles. Hour after hour, streaks of lightening lit up the sky.

The oak was old and weak by now, and had no brothers or sisters to lend strength in numbers. Try as it might to cling to the earth, it couldn't withstand the force of the howling winds.

Suddenly, with a giant shiver and shake, its roots gave way, and the poor old tree came crashing down.

 Once again, the seasons came and went, and the bones of the tree slowly, soundlessly, melted into the welcoming arms of the forest floor.

Chapter 2
Baby Beetles

Years later, voices of men could once again be heard in the woods. This time, though, they hadn't come to cut down a forest, but to plant one.

The tree hadn't lived long enough to see it, but the hearts of men had turned from greed to charity. Thousands of trees were planted in the forgotten woods, and the seeds of hope began to sprout.

The seasons changed just as they always had. Full moon and new, spring and

fall, year upon year passed once again, and once again, the forest quietly grew.

One clear, bright, early summer morning, a green beetle scrambled over what was left of the old oak tree.

Sunlight danced through the woods, but she couldn't stop to admire the beautiful scenery. She climbed to the ground, and poked through the decayed leaves until she found the entrance to her burrow. Soon she was snuggled deep in the earth.

The time had come for her to lay her eggs.

It was cool in the woods, and Mama Beetle was well prepared. She had carefully spent many months building her underground home full of tunnels and chambers. These buried rooms would keep her eggs safe from weather and predators.

One by one, she placed an egg in each room, and gave each egg a name. She named the very last egg, "Benjamin."

Mama Beetle cleaned and swept her home each day, patiently waiting for the eggs to hatch.

Finally, on a mid-summer day, she heard a scratching noise coming from one of the tunnels. She hurried to the sound, and there before her eyes was the most wonderful sight in the world.

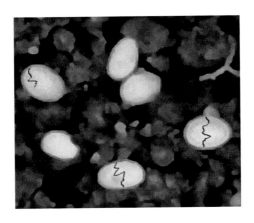

An egg had hatched! And then another! And another!

Soon the burrow was filled with baby grub worms. Mama Beetle joyfully counted each one, and suddenly realized someone was missing. Where was Benjamin? She hurried to his room, and there was the littlest egg, still sound asleep.

"Benjamin, wake up!" she said.
But Benny slept on.
Days passed in the burrow. Happy babies wiggled and crawled through the tunnels, stretching their little legs and chewing on the leaves Mama had provided. Her grubs were growing fast!

She kept a watchful eye on her last little egg.

"What is keeping that boy?" she wondered. He should be awake by now!

But still . . . Benny slept on.

At long last, the morning came when she heard a small scratching sound coming from Benny's room. She scurried to investigate, and before her eyes, out popped one little foot, and then another. Benny had finally hatched!

Mama Beetle washed his face and feet, and gently placed him near the tunnel door. Benny crawled up the hallway and out of the nest, and gazed for the first time on a beautiful forest world.

His brothers and sisters were used to being outside, and they were having fun eating and playing beetle games. They especially liked to lie on their backs and play upside-down inchworm.

Benny was so much littler, he was afraid to join in, so they didn't pay much attention to their youngest brother who was finally awake.

He might have been small, but boy was Benny hungry! He took a bite from a rotten old pine branch, and it was good! He ate til his tummy was full, and then inched his way back down  underground, crawled into his bedroom, and fell fast asleep.

Chapter 3
Metamorphosis!

 Benny grew bigger day by day. There was plenty to eat, and he munched happily on the dead branches and leaves that were plentiful in the forest.

The air was filled with noises that he soon learned to recognize: the chattering of blue jays and cardinals, the cooing of doves, the pips of nuthatches and mice, the rushing music of a stream swollen from the previous day's rains.

He listened to the sound of the wind whistling high through the pine trees, and the

rumble of thunder on a stormy
night.

He listened to the buzzing
of dragonflies, and the sleepy
droning of bees on a hot
afternoon.

He was happy in the forest,
but sometimes he was restless,
too.

Once, he heard the sound
of a dog's bark echoing from far
away. He wondered where the

sound was coming from, and what the creature looked like who made it.

He wished he could fly, up through the trees, soaring above and beyond the woods of the Croatan.

His heart longed for adventure.

Benny's body was changing, but he was too busy being a grub worm to notice. Sometimes, his skin got so tight around his body, he had to wiggle and wriggle and roll right out of it.

Mama Beetle watched her little bug, knowing that it wouldn't be long now before he would change in a very mysterious way.

One day, in the heat of summer, Benny had a sudden urge to build a fort. He gathered bits of wood and leaves, and pasted them together with mud. His fort

grew bigger as the day grew
hotter.

Finally he was able to
climb inside, but the sun was so
bright it hurt his eyes. He kept
working until the fort was
completely closed in, and by the
time he was done, he was
exhausted.

He closed his eyes to take a
little nap . . . and fell into a
deep, dreamless sleep.

More than three weeks
went by before he woke up. He
sat up with a start, trying to
remember where he was. It
was so dark in the fort that he
couldn't see a thing. He nibbled
the door open and squirmed
out.

As Benny yawned and
stretched, much to his surprise,
he realized something amazing

had happened – he no longer
looked like a little worm, and
his body was covered with a
hard, shiny green shell.

He moved his arms, and
out popped wings! Benny
realized he could fly!
He couldn't wait for his
first adventure!

Chapter 4
Flash

Benny's mother watched him grow with patience and love, as all good mothers do. His brothers and sisters were grown and gone, but Benny was still too little to be off by himself.

One day, he asked if he could go outside to play. Mama Beetle was very busy, and didn't have time to watch over him. He begged and pleaded, and finally she relented, making him promise not to leave the meadow.

Benny stepped outside cautiously, one foot at a time,

until his whole body was bathed
in the late afternoon sunshine.
He looked around at his forest
playground, trying to decide
which way to go first. He saw
an opening in the ferns that led
to the meadow, and off he flew.

He was a little bit clumsy
at first – flying was harder than
it looked! His wings carried
him higher and higher, and
soon he was racing from one
end of the meadow to the other.
　　Mama Beetle smiled as she
watched him. "Remember to

stay close to home," she said. "The forest is a big place, and it's easy to lose your way!"

She went inside to finish her cleaning, happy to see him having so much fun on his first day alone in the big world.

Benny flew back and forth through the meadow, more sure of himself with each pass, until he finally realized he was really tired. He wasn't used to so much flying and looking at new things! He had just landed in a patch of hydrangea flowers to rest, when suddenly  out popped a big bumble bee, angry at the intrusion.

Benny was so startled, he nearly collided with a dragonfly as he darted away. In his panic, he forgot to notice which way he was going. Soon he was deep in the forest, without a clue how to find his way home.

His heart was still thumping when he finally landed to rest. He had no idea where he was, and it was growing darker by the minute as the sun sank lower in the sky.

Benny looked around at his unfamiliar surroundings, and whimpered softly, "Mama, where are you?" But his voice fell to the ground, unanswered. His mother was too far away to hear her little bug's sad cry.

But happily, someone *had* heard! For just as it was time

for some bugs to go in at sunset,
for others it was time to come
out and play.

A young firefly, buzzing
around in his backyard, had
heard the peculiar noise coming
from nearby.

He landed on a branch and
listened closely, trying to figure
out what had made the sound.
It wasn't like anything he'd
ever heard before.

He waited patiently until
he heard it again. Being a very
curious little firefly, he decided

to go investigate.

He flew in the direction of the sound, trying to find its source, but it had stopped. He was just about to go back home when he heard it again: "Mama, where are you?"

He zoomed down to the forest floor, and saw a little green beetle sitting on a rock. He flew up to him and asked, "What are you?"

"I'm a green beetle bug!" Benny answered. "My name is Benny. What are you?"

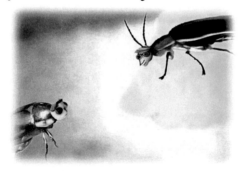

"I'm Flash, and I'm a firefly. Why are you crying?"

"I'm crying because I'm lost," Benny said. "This is my first day outside alone, and a giant black and yellow monster chased me into the woods. I don't know how to find my way home, and I know Mama will be really mad at me for not doing what she told me to do."

"I can help you if you want," said Flash.

"How?" Benny asked. "It's almost dark and I can barely see."

"Watch this!" Flash said, and he flew in a circle around Benny with a glow so bright it almost hurt Benny's eyes.

"How did you do that?" Benny asked in surprise.

"I'm a firefly! I glow in the dark!" Flash replied. "Come on,

let's go!" and off they flew, with
Flash leading the way.

Mama Beetle, preoccupied
with her chores, suddenly
realized it was nearly dark.
She went outside and looked for
Benny, but she didn't see him
anywhere.

She climbed to the top of
her porch and called, "Benny,
it's time to come home!" But
there was no reply.

She went to the meadow
and called again, louder this
time, "Benny, it's getting late,
time to come inside!"

But Benny was not in the meadow. He wasn't in the small thicket of dogwoods, or in the cherry tree that shaded their home; in fact he wasn't anywhere at all.

"Where could my little beetle bug be?" she cried. She flew as high as she could go, anxiously calling his name and buzzing around in circles.

Soon Benny could hear his mother, and his heart jumped in his chest. "Mama!" he called out, and she flew like an arrow straight to her little bug.

"Benny, you gave me a fright!" she said, relieved.

"Don't worry, Mrs. June Bug, I'm Benny's new friend," said Flash. "I'll make sure he gets home safe from now on."

Mama Beetle gave Flash a little hug and peck on the cheek.

"Thank you Flash, I'm so glad to know Benny has found such a good friend. You're welcome to come over anytime!"

"Thank you, Ma'am. Now I'd better get home before my Mama gets worried about me!" said Flash, and off he flew, like a, well, like a flash!

Chapter 5
Owl-fred

Benny grew bigger every day as the summer rolled slowly by. He couldn't wait to go outside to see what each new morning would bring.

He and Flash had become best friends. Each day, they would meet in a small patch of ferns that sprouted up under the pink dogwood trees. They spent most mornings chasing each other through the woods like the playful little bugs they were. In the afternoon heat, they would sit in the cool shade of an old pine tree stump, watching everyone come and go.

So many different kinds of creatures lived in the woods, and Benny couldn't wait to meet them all. On most days, they saw deer, wild turkeys, and rabbits. Sometimes, a fox or a stray hunting dog lost from his pack would wander by.

Birds chattered as they searched for food, or stopped to drink and bathe in the little stream that flowed through the meadow. It always made Benny laugh when he  watched them splash and shake and hop around in the water.

He didn't like it much when he had to take a bath!

Mama made him promise to always be home before dark, but it was hard to leave when he and Flash were having so much fun.

They soon learned the sounds that each bird made. They were all different, but in some ways the same; the happy little chirps of the redbirds and chickadees, the mouse-like squeaks of the hummingbirds, and the cooing of doves, all blended together into a forest symphony.

The Rufous Towhee sounded like he was always saying, "For meeee, for meeee." Benny thought he sounded very selfish, until Flash told him that Rufous was really saying, "To weeee, to weeee."

That sounded more like he was thinking of his friends too, so Benny decided Rufous was actually pretty nice.

Sometimes they heard the chirr-chirrhing echo of a red-tailed hawk, calling from far above the tall trees.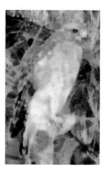

One evening, just as the first stars were beginning to twinkle in a purple sky, and Benny knew he should be going home, there was a sound that neither of them had ever heard before.

It sounded like a bird, but like something else, too.

Something that, maybe, shouldn't live in their safe and happy forest.

The hairs on Benny's neck stood up, and he let out a little gasp of surprise.

Flash jumped up and raced around in a circle, flashlight set on steady rather than the blink, blink he normally used.

"What was *that*?" he squeaked.

"I don't know!" Benny managed to reply, although he was having a hard time speaking.

"Let's find out!" said Flash.

Benny was definitely *not* happy about that idea. He secretly thought Flash was much braver than he was, but he was afraid of looking like a scaredy cat in front of his best friend.

"I think maybe I should go home now," he said. "It's getting dark!"

"OK," said Flash, "But let's go in the direction of that noise!"

Flash raced off before Benny could reply. He couldn't just Not Go, so he followed, a little distance behind, keeping Flash in his sights.

The woods were quiet. Benny was almost sure they had imagined the sound, when the deepening shadows were suddenly blasted again.

"Crikey!" Benny gasped. "Maybe we don't *want* to know what made that sound!" But Flash was more resolved than ever to find out what it was.

Up and up he flew, with Benny struggling behind, until they could both see the roof of an old barn, silhouetted in the glow of twilight.

"There! That's where the

sound is coming from!" cried Flash, and he took off like, well, you know.

Benny raced as fast as his little wings could go, trying to keep up. He'd lost sight of Flash, but he couldn't stop now! As he buzzed around the corner of the barn, he let out a little sigh of relief. There was Flash, hovering just outside the giant, inky black entrance to the dilapidated building.

They landed on an old red barn door that had fallen on the ground. Benny did *not* want to go inside, but he could tell from Flash's excitement that there was no way he could change his mind.

"Come on Benny, let's go see what's in there!" Flash

whispered. "Then we can go home."

"OK, but you first," Benny whispered back. "It's so dark I can't see anything."

And without another word, the adventurous little firefly darted into the blackness.

All was quiet inside the barn. Benny could barely make out shapes in the shadows cast by Flash's little blinking light. He hurried to keep up, not wanting the trusty light to disappear.

Just as he was about to catch up to Flash, the sound split the darkness again, and Benny's heart nearly stopped in his chest.

Two giant, yellow eyes were slowly blinking, right above their heads.

They both stopped in mid-air, mesmerized by the sight in front of them.

"Who, who, who are you" Benny managed to stutter.

"Who indeed?" answered a voice from the deep.

"Are you a monster?" asked Flash.

"No, no!" the voice replied. "I'm Owl-fred. I'm a Great Horned owl, and this is my barn! You are both very brave to be in here. Most creatures are too afraid to visit me, especially at this time of the day," said Owl-fred.

"Oh, we ARE very brave," said Flash, and Benny was happy to hear his friend thought *he* was brave, too.

"What are your names?" asked Owl-fred, scooting into the dim light coming in from a small window.

"I'm Flash, and this is Benny. We can't stay because

it's getting late, and Benny
can't see too good after dark.
He doesn't have a built-in
flashlight like me."

Owl-fred took out his
pocket watch to check the time.
"Yes," he said, "It is getting
late. You'd better hurry home
then. But you can come back
and visit any time you like."
"Thank you," said Benny.
"We will!" said Flash, and
off the two friends flew as fast

as their wings could go, straight to Benny's house.

Mama was waiting at the front door. With a sigh and with a little scold, she shooed Benny inside.

That night, tucked safely in his beetle bug bed, Benny remembered Owl-fred's words about how brave he and Flash were. He couldn't wait to see what adventures tomorrow would bring, as he drifted off to sleep.

Chapter 6
Pirates

Benny and Flash went to visit Owl-fred many times that summer. He was patient with their many questions, having been young once himself. They never ran out of questions to ask, because Owl-fred was as wise as a, well, you know.

One afternoon, the bugs were sitting on their favorite tree stump near Benny's house, when they heard a big crashing boom coming from a stand of trees off in the distance.

Curious little bugs that they were, they rushed to the place where they thought the sound came from. When they arrived, they could see that a huge limb had fallen from a tall poplar tree, and landed on the ground below.

The force of the blow had knocked over a rock, and the bugs could see that something was very peculiar about that rock. They couldn't figure out what it was, but they knew who they could ask.

As quickly as their little wings could carry them, they raced to the old barn to see if Owl-fred was awake. He slept mostly during the day, so they knew not to startle him when he was napping. They flew up to his favorite spot, with Flash as usual leading the way.

"Owl-fred," Benny said as soft as he could, given his excited state. "Are you awake?"

"I am now," said a sleepy voice from the blackness.

Owl-fred opened his big, yellow eyes, one at a time, and peered at his little friends.

"What's all the flap about?" he asked. "I can tell by your faces something more than boredom has brought you here!"

"Guess what!" Flash said,

eagerly. "We found something and we can't tell what it is, but it looks important. Come and see!"

Before Owl-fred could stretch his massive wings, off the two bugs flew.

"Wait up!" cried Owl-fred. "You two are so little even I have a hard time seeing you!"

He swooped down from the heights of the barn, and the three flew off into the forest.

"Here it is. Look, it's a big

rock, and it has funny looking squiggles all over it," said Benny.

Owl-fred landed on a pile of rubble just beside the rock, and studied it intently.

"It's not a rock," he said. "It's a tombstone."

"What's a tombstone?" asked Flash. "It looks like a plain old rock to me."

"Well, tombstones are usually made from stone, just like rocks are," Owl-fred explained. "But it's a special kind of rock. The people who share this forest with us, the kind that walk on two legs, use these rocks as a way of marking the place where one of them has been buried."

"Why would they do that?" asked Benny.

50

"Well," said Owl-fred, "When someone dies, the people who cared about them put their body in the ground, and set one of these special rocks on top so they don't forget where they've been laid to rest."

"Those two-legged people do the weirdest things," said Flash.

Benny thought the same thing. He was trying very hard to listen to Owl-fred, just like Mama taught him to, but he didn't understand at all. He wondered what Owl-fred meant by "when someone dies". He had never heard those words before, and what did "laid to rest" mean?

Before he could ask, Owl-fred said something even stranger.

"Listen! This is what it says," and he began to read the funny squiggles.

"Here be the body of Cap'n Will, the scurvy dog what parleyed with the dev'l, never his bones do stir. In the Lords Year, 1727."

Owl-fred's eyes got even bigger than they usually were.

"Holy smokes," he said excitedly. "Boys, I think you

found the final resting place of Captain William Lewis!"

"Wow!" Flash cried. He buzzed up and down in place, then stopped suddenly. "What's a cap'n?"

"Well, many, many years ago, the waters around these parts were full of pirates. They were ruthless scoundrels who robbed the ships of law-abiding sailors and sometimes other pirates," said Owl-fred.

"They were greatly feared, but the most feared of all the pirates was the captain of the ship. He gave the orders, and his crew did what he said, or suffered the consequences."

Those were a lot more words that Benny didn't understand, but it all sounded very important. Flash was buzzing around the ground, and before Owl-fred could say "Shiver me timbers!" he had disappeared down a hole that was uncovered when the tombstone toppled over.

Benny scurried after him, down, down, down into that dark hole, watching Flash's little beam of light blink on and off, on and off. He had almost caught up with Flash when he heard him give a shout.

"Benny, come quick, look what I found!"

"I'm right behind you, Flash. What did you find?" asked Benny.

"I don't know," Flash replied. "Help me pull it out!"

The two little bugs pulled and tugged on a leather pouch

that was rolled up tight, tied
with a small string. It was
stuck inside the
pocket of an old
jacket that had
collapsed on top
of a pile of bones.
They finally got
one piece of the
string free, and
between the two

of them, were able to get it up
near the surface.

Owl-fred was waiting to
help them pull it the rest of the
way. He clutched it in his big
toes and got it clear of the hole.
Grabbing the string with his
pointy beak, he gave it a quick
tug.

The pouch rolled open, and
a clump of what looked like dirt

fell out. It smelled funny, but not in a bad sort of way. "Owl-fred, what kind of dirt is that?" asked Flash.

"It's not dirt, it's a wad of old tobacco," Owl-fred replied. "And look at the inside of the pouch! Boys, I believe we've found a treasure map!"

What's a treasure map?" Benny asked, timidly. All this talk about dangerous men and someone called the dev'l had made him just a bit nervous.

"Pirates were infamous scallywags and thieves. They worried about other pirates trying to steal from them what they had stolen from others," said Owl-fred. "Sometimes they had to hide their ill-gotten booty, and go back for it later.

They used a map like this to remember where it was."

The three friends studied the map intently.

"It looks like Cap'n Will drew this map inside his tobacco pouch to hide it from prying eyes," said Owl-fred.

"If the legend is true, his crew believed he had made a deal with the devil. Pirates were very superstitious, and fearing for their souls, they murdered him one night in his sleep. They must've been in such a hurry to bury him, they didn't want to search his clothes for anything of value."

"Do you think we should go look for the treasure?" asked Flash. He was a very curious firefly, after all.

"It's probably very far from here," said Owl-fred, "Too far for a little bug to fly. And even if we did find it, there wouldn't be any way for us to get the treasure home. But I think we should keep the map. It might come in handy later."

The three agreed that Owl-fred should take it to his barn, since it was too big for either bug to keep at their house.

The sun was just starting

to set as the trio of friends flew back home, Owl-fred clutching the map in his huge feet. They talked about Cap'n Will, and pirates, and treasure maps, and about the strange things people would sometimes do.

But most of all, they agreed how very fortunate they were to live in the remarkable place called the *Croatan Woods*.

What do you suppose the friends will be up to next? Do you think they noticed the little ladybug who saw them discover the treasure map?

Look for more *Adventures of Benny and Flash,* coming soon!

Made in the USA
San Bernardino, CA
11 September 2016